A Note to Parents

DK READERS is a compelling programme for beginning readers, designed in conjunction with leading literacy

the class.

Beautiful illustrations and superb full-colour photograph.. combine with engaging, easy-to-read stories to offer a fresh approach to each subject in the series. Each DK READER is guaranteed to capture a child's interest while developing his or her reading skills, general knowledge and love of reading.

The five levels of DK READERS are aimed at different reading abilities, enabling you to choose the books that are exactly right for your child:

Pre-level 1: Learning to read

Level 1: Beginning to read

Level 2: Beginning to read alone

Level 3: Reading alone

Level 4: Proficient readers

The "normal" age at which a child begins to read can be anywhere from three to eight years old. Adult participation through the lower levels is very helpful for providing encouragement, discussing storylines and sounding out unfamiliar words.

No matter which level you select, you can be sure tha~ ~~~ child lea~~ to

LONDON, NEW YORK, MELBOURNE,
MUNICH AND DELHI

For Dorling Kindersley
Editor Lucy Dowling
Designer Dan Bunyan
Managing Editor Catherine Saunders
Art Director Lisa Lanzarini
Publishing Manager Simon Beecroft
Category Publisher Alex Allan
Production Editor Siu Yin Chan
Production Controller Nick Seston

For LucasFilm
Executive Editor Jonathan W. Rinzler
Art Director Troy Alders
Keeper of the Holocron Leland Chee
Director of Publishing Carol Roeder

Reading Consultant
Maureen Fernandes

First published in Great Britain in 2010 by
Dorling Kindersley Limited
80 Strand, London WC2R 0RL

A CIP catalogue record for this book
is available from the British Library.

ISBN: 978-1-40534-337-4

Colour reproduction by Alta Images
Printed and bound in China by L.Rex

Discover more at
www.dk.com
www.starwars.com

DK READERS

BEGINNING

1

TO READ

STAR WARS®

THE CLONE WARS™

Pirates...
And Worse!

Written by Simon Beecroft

This is Hondo Ohnaka
and his scary gang.
They are all space pirates.

They attack spaceships
and steal treasure.

Hondo is the leader of the gang.

He wears goggles and a stolen overcoat.

Hondo makes sure every pirate receives his share of the treasure.

Turk Falso is in Hondo's gang.

He is second-in-command.

Turk Falso thinks he is much
smarter than Hondo.
He always tries to outwit Hondo.

Pilf Mukmuk is the pirates'
monkey-lizard.
He hops from pirate
shoulder to pirate shoulder.
He does sneaky little jobs
for the pirates.

But when the pirates are
asleep, he steals from them!

The rest of the pirate gang is a
ragtag bunch of villains.
They have rough, wrinkled skin.

One pirate has a metal peg-leg.
They argue a lot and sometimes
they even fight each other!

The pirates have a big spaceship. They fly through space looking for other ships to attack.

Other pilots dread seeing the big red pirate symbol on the wing of Hondo's ship.
It means trouble!

Symbol

After a successful raid, the pirates return to their secret base. To celebrate, they have a feast.

The pirates eat and drink.
They play noisy games and
dance on the tabletops.

Hondo and his gang
fight anyone who
tries to attack them.
They drive around in
big tanks that float
above the ground.
Nobody can steal
Hondo's stolen treasure!

Tank

Watch out! The pirates also ride around on flying speeder bikes.

These bikes can fly really fast.
If a ship crash-lands on their
planet, Hondo's gang arrive
quickly and find things to steal.

Speeder Bike

The pirates capture a spaceship
that belongs to Count Dooku,
a powerful Sith Lord.
Count Dooku goes to fight them.

But he cannot
find his lightsaber.
The pirates have
already stolen it!

Sith

The pirates know that some Jedi
are looking for Count Dooku.
So they capture Dooku and
demand a high ransom.

Jedi

Suddenly, Jedi Knights Anakin
and Obi-Wan appear.
But the cunning pirates capture
them too!

Senator Jar Jar Binks comes to give the ransom to the pirates.

Hondo sends Turk Falso to meet the Senator.
But Turk Falso wants the money for himself, so he attacks Jar Jar Binks' ship.

While Turk is busy fighting
Jar Jar, Anakin and Obi-Wan
manage to escape.

Then the two Jedi Knights
capture the pirate
leader, Hondo.

Hondo realises Turk
Falso has betrayed him.

The Jedi let Hondo go.
Count Dooku also escapes.
The Jedi warn the pirates
that Dooku will want revenge.

Hondo has learned that the only thing worse than a pirate... is an angry Sith Lord!

Glossary

Symbol
A shape that represents an organisation or group

Tank
A battle vehicle with large guns

Speeder Bike
A powered flying vehicle

Sith
A member of a group with evil powers

Jedi
A member of a group with powers for good